THE WIND IN THE WILLOWS

The Adventures of Mr. Toad

Re-told by Anne McKie. Illustrated by Ken McKie.

It was a bright morning in the early part of summer and the Mole and the Water Rat had been up since dawn, very busy getting ready for the boating season.

They were finishing breakfast in their little parlour and eagerly discussing their plans for the day, when a heavy knock sounded at the door.

"Bother!" said the Rat, egg all over him. "See who it is, Mole, like a good fellow, since you've finished."

The Mole went to answer the door, and Rat heard him utter a cry of surprise, "It's Mr. Badger!"

Now Badger never ever called to see anyone - so this must be a call of some importance.

The Badger strode heavily into the room looking very serious. The Rat let his egg spoon fall on the table cloth and sat open-mouthed.

"The hour has come!" said the Badger, "to do something about Toad! I learned last night," he continued, "that another new and very powerful motor car will arrive at Toad Hall today."

Now all three friends had to agree that they simply must put a stop to Toad's hopelessly bad driving. They had lost count of the cars he had crashed and the fines he had paid.

"He'll be ruined or killed or both," said Ratty. "Badger! We are his friends, we ought to do something!"

So they set off up the road to Toad Hall, to find as the Badger had expected, a shiny new motor car of great size - painted a bright red - standing in front of the house.

As they neared the door it was flung open, and Mr. Toad, dressed in goggles, cap, gaiters and enormous overcoat, came swaggering down the steps, pulling on his gloves.

The Badger strode up the steps. "Take him inside," he said sternly to Rat and Mole. Then, as Toad was hustled through the door, struggling and protesting, Badger turned to the chauffeur in charge of the new motor car.

"I'm afraid you won't be wanted today," he said. "Mr. Toad has changed his mind. He will not require the car!"

"Now then!" he said to Toad, when the four of them stood together in the hall, "first of all take those ridiculous things off!"

"Shan't!" replied Toad with great spirit.

"Take them off him, then, you two," ordered the Badger briefly.

Toad kicked and yelled and called them all sorts of names. The Rat sat on him, and Mole got his motor-clothes off him bit by bit, and they stood him up on his legs again.

"You knew it must come to this, sooner or later, Toad," the Badger explained severely. "You're getting us a bad name by your furious driving and your smashes and your rows with the police."

Then Badger took Toad into another room and gave him a real talking-to. After almost an hour he came out with a very sorry looking Toad.

"My friends," said Badger, "I'm pleased to tell you that Toad is truly sorry for his bad behaviour, and has promised to give up motor cars for ever."

There was a long pause. Toad looked this way and that. At last he spoke, "I am not sorry. Motor cars are simply wonderful! In fact, I promise that the very first one I see, off I shall go in it!"

"Very well then," said Badger firmly. "We shall lock you upstairs in your room until this silly craze for motor cars is over!"

So poor Toad, kicking and struggling, was hauled upstairs by his three faithful friends.

As Mole turned the key on him and went downstairs, Toad shouted abuse through the keyhole.

"I've never seen Toad so determined," said Badger. "He must never be left for an instant, until he has forgotten all about those stupid motor cars!"

They arranged to keep watch over him. Each animal took it in turns to sleep in Toad's room, and they divided up the day between them.

One fine morning, it was Rat's turn to be on duty. He found Toad still in bed saying he was far too ill to get up.

"Go to the village and fetch the doctor, Ratty!" murmured Toad feebly, "before it's too late!"

The Water Rat was very alarmed and hurried from the room, locked the door behind him and ran off to the village.

The Toad, who had hopped lightly out of bed as soon as he heard the key turn in the lock, watched him eagerly from the window till he disappeared down the drive.

Then, laughing heartily, he dressed as quickly as possible, and, knotting the sheets from his bed together, he scrambled out of the window and slid to the ground. And, taking the opposite direction to Rat, marched off light-heartedly, whistling a merry tune.

How gloomy the three friends felt, when Rat admitted to Mole and Badger just how easily he had been taken in by Toad.

How conceited Toad looked as he strode along, his head in the air, thinking to himself how clever he was outsmarting poor old Ratty!

Soon he was miles away from Toad Hall, and beginning to feel very hungry. He stopped at the first inn he found and ordered the best meal they had.

Toad was halfway through his meal when he heard a familiar sound that made him jump and tremble all over.

A motor car turned into the yard and came to a stop. The driver got out and called into the inn for a meal. All of a sudden, Toad had a splendid idea! He paid his bill, slipped quietly out of the inn, and went straight round to the yard. "There can't be any harm in just looking at it!"

The car stood in the middle of the yard. No one was there! Toad walked slowly around it. "I wonder if this sort of car starts easily?"

Next moment, hardly knowing how it happened, he had turned the starting handle and jumped into the driver's seat. As if in a dream, he swung the car round the yard and drove off through the archway.

Soon he was speeding along the highway and out into the open country. Faster and faster Toad went, not knowing where he was going, nor caring what might happen to him.

Sad to say the worst did happen! Toad found himself in court. There he was standing trembling all alone in the dock, a policeman either side of him. Poor Toad! No one to help him get out of this mess, and his dear friends, Ratty, Mole and Badger, miles away.

The court found Toad guilty of stealing a valuable motor car, dangerous driving and being rude to the police. Worse was to come! They sent Toad to prison for twenty years!

The poor fellow was handcuffed to two policemen and dragged, shrieking and screaming, across the market-place into a grim old castle, which was to be his prison.

Toad was taken down the steps to the deepest dungeon they could find.

"Guard this villainous criminal with your life!" one of the policemen ordered the old gaoler who was put in charge of Toad.

The gaoler nodded as he put Toad inside his cell. The rusty key turned in the lock, the great door clanged behind him, and Toad was a helpless prisoner.

Alone and locked away in a damp and dark dungeon, Toad flung himself on the floor and shed bitter tears of despair.

"This is the end of everything," cried the unhappy Toad. "This is the end of the career of Toad, the popular, handsome Toad, the rich and hospitable Toad! How can I ever hope to be free again? Oh, unhappy and forsaken Toad!"

He was so miserable, he cried all day and all night. He refused all the meals the gaoler brought to him, he was so busy feeling sorry for himself.

Now the gaoler had a pretty and kind-hearted daughter who was very fond of animals. Because she couldn't bear seeing Toad so unhappy, she begged her father to let her look after the poor animal.

"Now, cheer up, Toad," she said as she unlocked his cell. "Sit up and dry your eyes and be a sensible animal. And do try to eat a bit of dinner!"

But Toad still wailed, kicked his legs and refused to be comforted.

So the wise girl went away, but she left the plate of hot food, which to the hungry Toad, smelt very appetising. Between mouthfuls and sniffs and sobs, Toad began to cheer up - just a little!

When the girl came back a few hours later, she carried a tray with fresh tea and a plate of hot, buttered toast.

Toad sat up, dried his eyes, sipped his tea and munched his toast, and pretty soon began to boast about himself, his grand house and how important he was!

He told the gaoler's daughter all about Toad Hall and about his friends, Ratty, Mole and Badger, and all of the fun they had together at home.

The girl and Toad had many interesting talks together, as the dreary days went on, the girl grew very sorry for Toad. She hated seeing a poor little animal being locked up at all, for what seemed to her to be a very small crime.

"Toad," said the gaoler's daughter, one morning. "I have an aunt who is a washerwoman. She does washing for all the prisoners in this castle, and she will be coming here tomorrow to return this week's washing."

The girl took a long look at Toad. "You look quite like her - especially your figure! If she would let you have her dress and bonnet, you could escape dressed as a washerwoman!"

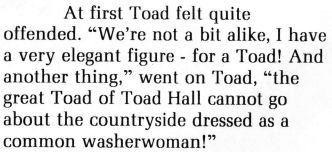

At first Toad felt quite offended. "We're not a bit alike, I have a very elegant figure - for a Toad! And another thing," went on Toad, "the great Toad of Toad Hall cannot go about the countryside dressed as a common washerwoman!"

"Then you can stop in prison, you ungrateful Toad!" replied the girl.

At once Toad felt sorry he had sounded so rude. "You are a good, kind, clever girl," he said, "and I am a proud and stupid Toad. Please introduce me to your aunt, so that she might help me."

The very next evening the girl took her aunt to Toad's cell. Inside the bundle of washing she had carefully hidden a cotton gown, an apron, a shawl and a black bonnet.

First they tied the old lady up - just so no one would think that she helped Toad to escape. Quickly, Toad took off his coat and waistcoat and put on the gown and shawl. The gaoler's daughter shook with laughter as she tied the strings of the black bonnet under Toad's chin.

"Now, goodbye, Toad, and good luck - be careful going past the guards!"

With a quaking heart Toad set off. It all seemed so easy.
Not one sentry stopped him! He looked so much like the
washerwoman that every guard let him pass.

At last he heard the great prison door clang shut behind
him, he felt the fresh air on his face and knew that he was free!

Dizzy with the success of his daring escape, he walked
quickly towards the nearest town.

As he went along he heard the
sound of the puffing and snorting of
engines. "This is a piece of luck,"
thought Toad, "a railway station!"

He looked at the timetable, and
found, to his delight, that a train was
going very near Toad hall in half-an-
hour. So off he went to the booking
office to buy his ticket.

He felt in his pocket for the money, when, to his horror, he remembered he had left his waistcoat and jacket and all his money in the prison cell.

"Look here!" said Toad rather grandly, to the man in the ticket office. "I have left my purse behind. Give me a ticket and I will send the money to you!"

"Indeed you will not," snapped the man. "Get away from the window, you are blocking the other passengers!"

Full of despair, Toad wandered blindly down the platform to where the train was standing, tears trickled down each side of his nose.

Very soon his escape would be discovered, the prison guards would hunt him down, they would drag him back again and feed him on bread and water!

Suddenly, Toad found himself opposite the engine, which was being oiled and cleaned by its driver.

"Hello there!" said the man, "what's the trouble?"

"Oh, sir!" said Toad, crying again. "I am a poor washerwoman, I've lost all my money, and can't pay for my ticket. I must get home at once to my poor innocent children," sobbed Toad.

"I'll tell you what," said the engine driver. "My shirts get awful dirty on this engine. If you promise to wash me a few when you get home, you can ride up on the engine!"

Toad's misery turned to rapture, although he had never washed a shirt in his life, and didn't intend to!

The guard waved the flag, the whistle blew, and the train moved out of the station. As the speed increased, Toad thought how every minute was bringing him nearer Toad Hall. He was so happy, he began to skip up and down and sing.

They had travelled many a mile, when Toad noticed a puzzled expression on the engine driver's face. "I could swear there was another train behind us!"

Toad stopped his singing at once and began to feel afraid.

By now the moon was shining brightly and the driver could see quite clearly that they were being followed. "They're gaining on us fast!" cried the engine driver. "It's full of policemen with truncheons and detectives waving revolvers and walking sticks; all waving and shouting the same thing - 'Stop! Stop! Stop!'"

Then Toad fell on his knees among the coals. "Save me, save me, dear, kind Mr. Engine Driver," he pleaded. "I will confess everything! I am not the simple washerwoman I seem to be! I have no children waiting for me. I am the well known and popular Mr. Toad; I have just escaped, by great daring and cleverness, from a grim and dark prison cell. If those fellows on that engine recapture me, they will fling me straight back in there!"

The engine driver looked very grave and said, "I fear that you have been a very wicked Toad and, by rights, I ought to give you up. But as you are in trouble and distress I will not desert you."

Toad felt very relieved.

"I don't like motor cars very much," the driver went on, "and I don't like being ordered about by policemen when I'm on my own engine. So cheer up, Toad! I'll do my best, and we may beat them yet!"

They piled on more coals, shovelling furiously, the furnace roared, the sparks flew, the engine leapt and swung, but still the other engine slowly gained on them.

"It's no good, Toad!" sighed the driver, as he wiped his brow with a rag. "They have the better engine. There's just one thing left to do, so listen carefully to what I tell you. Straight ahead is a long tunnel with a thick wood at the end of it. Now I will put on speed as we are running through the tunnel (the other train will slow down for fear of an accident). When we are through, I will put on the brakes as hard as I can - then you must jump off and hide in the wood. Then I will go full speed ahead again, and they can chase me for as long as they like and as far as they like."

They piled on more coals and the train shot into the tunnel, once they were through the driver shut off steam and put on the brakes.

Toad got down on the step, and as the train slowed down almost to walking pace, he heard the driver call out, "now jump!"

Toad jumped, rolled down a short bank, picked himself up unhurt, scrambled into the wood and hid.

Peeping out, he saw his train pick up speed again and disappear at a great pace.

Then out of the tunnel burst the other engine, roaring and whistling, the policemen and guards waving their weapons and shouting, "Stop! Stop! Stop!"

When they were past, Toad had a good laugh, but he soon stopped when he realised how very late and dark and cold it was. There was he, in an unknown wood, far away from friends and home.

That night, a tired and hungry Toad slept in a hollow tree. However, he managed to make himself comfortable and slept soundly till the morning.

He was awakened at first light by a shaft of bright warm sunlight.

Sitting up, he rubbed his eyes, wondering for a moment where he was. "Oh, joy!" cried Toad, when he remembered he was no longer in prison - he was free!

But all Toad wanted, on that early summer's morning, was to get back to Toad Hall and his dear friends, Ratty, Mole and Badger.